A Party for
Winnie-the-Pooh

A.A. Milne

Illustrated by E.H. Shepard

EGMONT

One day when the sun had come back over the Forest,

bringing with it the scent of may, and all
the streams of the Forest were tinkling
happily to find themselves their own
pretty shape again, and the little pools
lay dreaming of the life they had seen
and the big things they had done, and in
the warmth and quiet of the Forest the
cuckoo was trying over his voice carefully
and listening to see if he liked it, and
wood-pigeons were complaining gently to
themselves in their lazy comfortable way
that it was the other fellow's fault, but it

didn't matter very much; on such a day as this Christopher Robin whistled in a special way he had, and Owl came flying out of the Hundred Acre Wood to see what was wanted.

'Owl,' said Christopher Robin, 'I am going to give a party.'

'You are, are you?' said Owl.

'And it's to be a special sort of party, because it's because of what Pooh did when he did what he did to save Piglet from the flood.'

'Oh, that's what it's for, is it?' said Owl.

'Yes, so will you tell Pooh as quickly as you can, and all the others, because it will be to-morrow?'

'Oh, it will, will it?' said Owl, still being as helpful as possible.

'So will you go and tell them, Owl?'

Owl tried to think of something very wise to say, but couldn't, so he flew off to tell the others. And the first person he told was Pooh.

'Pooh,' he said, 'Christopher Robin is giving a party.'

'Oh!' said Pooh. And then seeing that Owl expected him to say something else, he said, 'Will there be those little cake things with pink sugar icing?'

Owl felt that it was rather beneath him to talk about little cake things with pink sugar icing, so he told Pooh exactly what Christopher Robin had said, and flew off to Eeyore.

'A party for Me?' thought Pooh to
himself. 'How grand!' And he began to
wonder if all the other animals would
know that it was a special Pooh Party,

and if Christopher Robin had told
them about *The Floating Bear*
and the *Brain of Pooh* and all the
wonderful ships he had invented and
sailed on, and he began to think how
awful it would be if everybody had
forgotten about it, and nobody quite
knew what the party was for; and the
more he thought like this, the more
the party got muddled in his mind,
like a dream when nothing goes right.

And the dream began to sing itself over in his head until it became a sort of song. It was an

ANXIOUS

POOH

SONG

3 Cheers for Pooh!

(For who?)

For Pooh –

(Why what did he do?)

I thought you knew;

He saved his friend

from a wetting!

3 Cheers for Bear!

(For where?)

For Bear –

He couldn't swim,

But he rescued him!

(He rescued who?)

Oh, listen, do!

I am talking of Pooh —

(Of who?)

Of Pooh!

(I'm sorry I keep forgetting).

Well, Pooh was a Bear
        of Enormous Brain –
(Just say it again!)
            Of enormous brain –
(Of enormous what?)
                Well, he ate a lot,
And I don't know if he could
                swim or not,

But he managed to float

On a sort of boat

(On a sort of *what?*)

Well, a sort of pot –

So now let's give him
three hearty cheers

(So now let's give him
three hearty whiches!)

And hope he'll be with us
for years and years,

And grow in health and
wisdom and riches!

3 Cheers for Pooh!

(For who?)

For Pooh –

3 Cheers for Bear!

(For where?)

For Bear –

3 Cheers for the wonderful

Winnie-the-Pooh!

(Just tell me, somebody –

WHAT DID HE DO?)

While this was going on inside him,
Owl was talking to Eeyore.

'Eeyore,' said Owl, 'Christopher
Robin is giving a party.'

'Very interesting,' said Eeyore. 'I
suppose they will be sending me down
the odd bits which got trodden on.

Kind and Thoughtful. Not at all, don't mention it.'

'There is an Invitation for you.'

'What's that like?'

'An Invitation!'

'Yes, I heard you. Who dropped it?'

'This isn't anything to eat, it's asking you to the party. To-morrow.'

Eeyore shook his head slowly.

'You mean Piglet. The little fellow with the excited ears. That's Piglet. I'll tell him.'

'No, no!' said Owl, getting quite fussy.
'It's you!'

'Are you sure?'

'Of course I'm sure. Christopher
Robin said "All of them! Tell all of
them." '

'All of them, except Eeyore?'

'All of them,' said Owl sulkily.

'Ah!' said Eeyore. 'A mistake, no doubt, but still, I shall come. Only don't blame *me* if it rains.'

But it didn't rain. Christopher Robin had made a long table out of some long pieces of wood, and they all sat round it. Christopher Robin sat at one end, and Pooh sat at the other, and between them on one side were Owl and Eeyore and Piglet, and between them on the other side were Rabbit, and Roo and Kanga. And all Rabbit's friends and relations spread themselves about on the grass, and waited hopefully in case anybody spoke to them, or dropped anything, or asked them the time.

It was the first party to which Roo had ever been, and he was very excited. As soon as ever they had sat down he began to talk.

'Hallo, Pooh!' he squeaked.

'Hallo, Roo!' said Pooh.

Roo jumped up and down in his seat for a little while and then began again.

'Hallo, Piglet!' he squeaked.

Piglet waved a paw at him, being too busy to say anything.

'Hallo, Eeyore!' said Roo.

Eeyore nodded gloomily at him. 'It

will rain soon, you see if it doesn't,'
he said.

Roo looked to see if it didn't, and it
didn't, so he said 'Hallo, Owl!' – and
Owl said 'Hallo, my little fellow,' in
a kindly way, and went
on telling Christopher
Robin about an accident
which had nearly
happened to a friend of
his whom Christopher Robin
didn't know, and Kanga said to Roo,

'Drink up your milk first, dear, and talk afterwards.'

So Roo, who was drinking his milk,
tried to say that he could do both at
once . . . and had to be patted on the
back and dried for quite a long time
afterwards.

When they had all nearly eaten
enough, Christopher Robin banged on
the table with his spoon, and everybody
stopped talking and was very silent,
except Roo who was just finishing a loud
attack of hiccups and trying to look as if
it was one of Rabbit's relations.

'This party,' said Christopher Robin, 'is a party because of what someone did, and we all know who it was, and it's his party, because of what he did, and I've got a present for him and here it is.' Then he felt about a little and whispered, 'Where is it?'

While he was looking, Eeyore coughed in an impressive way and began to speak.

'Friends,' he said, 'including oddments, it is a great pleasure, or

perhaps I had better say it
has been a pleasure so
far, to see you at my
party. What I did was
nothing. Any of you –
except Rabbit and Owl and
Kanga – would have done the same.
Oh, and Pooh. My remarks do not, of
course, apply to Piglet and Roo,
because they are too small. Any of you
would have done the same. But it just
happened to be Me. It was not, I need

hardly say, with an idea of getting what Christopher Robin is looking for now' – and he put his front leg to his mouth and said in a loud whisper, 'Try under the table' – 'that I did what I did – but because I feel that we should all do what we can to help. I feel that we should all –'

'H–hup!' said Roo accidentally.

'Roo, dear!' said Kanga reproachfully.

'Was it me?' asked Roo, a little surprised.

'What's Eeyore
talking about?'
Piglet whispered
to Pooh.

'I don't know,'
said Pooh rather
dolefully.

'I thought this was *your* party.'

'I thought it was *once*. But I suppose
it isn't.'

'I'd sooner it was yours than Eeyore's,'
said Piglet.

'So would I,' said Pooh.

'H–hup!' said Roo again.

'AS – I – WAS – SAYING,' said Eeyore loudly and sternly, 'as I was saying when I was interrupted by various Loud Sounds, I feel that –'

'Here it is!' cried Christopher Robin excitedly. 'Pass it down to silly old Pooh. It's for Pooh.'

'For Pooh?' said Eeyore.

'Of course it is. The best bear in all the world.'

"Open it, Pooh"

'I might have known,' said Eeyore. 'After all, one can't complain. I have my friends. Somebody spoke to me only yesterday. And was it last week or the week before that Rabbit bumped into me and said "Bother!" The Social Round. Always something going on.'

Nobody was listening, for they were all saying, 'Open it, Pooh,' 'What is it, Pooh?' 'I know what it is,' 'No, you don't,' and other helpful remarks of this sort. And of course Pooh was opening it as quickly as ever he could, but without cutting the string, because you never know when a bit of string might be Useful. At last it was undone.

When Pooh saw what it was, he nearly fell down, he was so pleased. It was a Special Pencil Case

There were pencils in it marked

'B' for Bear,

and pencils marked

'HB' for Helping Bear,

and pencils marked

'BB' for Brave Bear.

There was a knife for sharpening the pencils, and india-rubber for rubbing out anything which you had spelt wrong, and a ruler for ruling lines for the words to walk on, and inches marked on the ruler in case you wanted to know how many inches anything was, and Blue Pencils and Red Pencils and Green Pencils for saying special things in blue and red and green. And all these lovely things were in little pockets of their own in a Special Case which shut with a click when you clicked it. And they were all for Pooh.

'Oh!' said Pooh.
'Oh, Pooh!' said
everybody else
except Eeyore.
'Thank-you,'
growled Pooh.

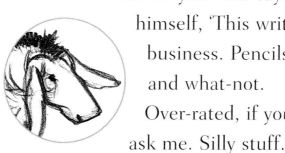

But Eeyore was saying to
himself, 'This writing
business. Pencils
and what-not.
Over-rated, if you
ask me. Silly stuff.

Nothing in it.'

Later on, when they had all said 'Good-bye' and 'Thank-you' to Christopher Robin, Pooh and Piglet walked home thoughtfully together in the golden evening, and for a long time they were silent.

'When you wake up in the morning, Pooh,' said Piglet at last, 'what's the first thing you say to yourself?'

'What's for breakfast?' said Pooh. 'What do *you* say, Piglet?'

'I say, I wonder what's going to
happen exciting *to-day*?' said Piglet.
Pooh nodded thoughtfully.
'It's the same thing,' he said.

*　　*　　*　　*　　*

'And what did happen?' asked
Christopher Robin.

'When?'

'Next morning.'

'I don't know.'

'Could you think, and tell me and
Pooh some time?'

'If you wanted it very much.'

'Pooh does,' said Christopher Robin.

He gave a deep sigh, picked his
bear up by the leg and walked off to

the door, trailing Winnie-the-Pooh
behind him. At the door he turned and
said,

'Coming to see me have my bath?'
  'I might,' I said.

'Was Pooh's pencil case any better than mine?'

'It was just the same,' I said.

He nodded and went out . . . and in a moment I heard Winnie-the-Pooh –

bump,
bump,
bump

– going up the stairs behind him.

A *Party for Winnie-the-Pooh*
is taken from *Winnie-the-Pooh*
originally published in
Great Britain 14 October 1926
by Methuen & Co. Ltd.
Text by A.A. Milne and line drawings by Ernest H. Shepard
copyright under the Berne Convention.

This edition published in Great Britain 2003
by Egmont Books Limited,
239 Kensington High Street, London W8 6SA.

1   3   5   7   9   10   8   6   4   2

Printed in China

ISBN 1 4052 0497 4